Does a Sea Cow Say MOO?

Terry Webb Harshman

illustrated by George McClements

BLOOMSBURY
CHILDREN'S
BOOKS

To my father, who showed his little girl the sea,
and to my brother Mick, who shared its wonders with me
– T. W. H.

For my beautiful mermaid, Rachel, and my guppies, Samuel and Matthew
– G. M.

First published in Great Britain in 2008 by Bloomsbury Publishing Plc,
36 Soho Square, London, W1D 3QY

First published in America in 2008 by Bloomsbury USA Children's Books
175 Fifth Avenue, New York, NY 10010

Text copyright © Terry Webb Harshman 2008
Illustrations copyright © George McClements 2008

A CIP catalogue record of this book is available from the British Library

ISBN 978 0 7475 8734 7

Printed and bound in China

10 9 8 7 6 5 4 3 2 1

All papers used by Bloomsbury Publishing are natural, recyclable products
made from wood grown in well-managed forests. The manufacturing processes
conform to the environmental regulations of the country of origin.

A spaceship touched down
On the beach with a *splash!*
The pilot saw Jack
And said, "My name's Flash!

I've come to find out
Why some names in the sea
Are the same as on land . . .
Will you please help me?"

"You need help, you say?
Then it's your lucky day!

My friends call me Jack,
And I'll be your guide
To some of the creatures
Who live in the tide!"

"SCHOOL in the sea.
SCHOOL in your town.
Does a school of fish study
In classrooms deep down?"

"In classrooms deep down?
Not with sharks circling round!

A school is when fishes
Go swimming in bunches;
Fish swimming solo
Can end up as lunches!"

"COW in the sea.
COW in the field.
Does a sea cow say *moo*
And eat grass for its meal?"

"A sea cow say *moo*?
No, that isn't true!

It chirps and it clicks
And it whistles instead,
And grazes on sea plants
In shallow seabeds."

"CLOWN in the sea.
CLOWN at the fair.
Do clown fish wear bow ties
And curly red hair?"

"Wear bow ties and hair?
This fish wouldn't dare!

Predators spot his
Bright colours with ease!
For protection he darts
In anemones."

"HORSE in the sea.
HORSE in the hay.
Can you saddle a sea horse
And gallop away?"

"Saddle a sea horse?
Not this fancy-free horse!

A small dorsal fin
Steers this miniature steed;
For safety he hitches
Himself to seaweed."

"BED in the sea.
BED where you sleep.
Is an oyster bed comfy?
Can you snuggle down deep?"

"Is an oyster bed comfy?
Oh no, it's quite lumpy!

It's a place just for shellfish,
Quite rocky and clammy,
Where oysters wear seashells
Instead of their jammies!"

"STAR in the sea.
STAR in the sky.
Do you wish on a starfish
As it whizzes by?"

"As it whizzes by?
This star's slow and shy!

It gracefully glides
On tiny tube feet,
Searching the tide pools
For a mollusc to eat."

"It's clear to me, Jack!
And thank you, my friend –
But I'm sad that my visit
Has come to an end."

"You really must go?
Well, if that is so,
Please come again, Flash,
And I'll show you more
Mysteries and wonders
That we can explore!"

Silly Sea Facts!

- **CLOWN FISH:** This bright little fish lives in coral reefs and among sea anemones (uh-NEM-uh-nees), which grow on the sea floor. When very young, it picks a poisonous sea anemone to get to know, brushing against it over and over again. Then, when an enemy appears, the clown fish escapes by darting into the stinging tentacles of its anemone "friend."

- **OYSTER BED:** An oyster bed is a rocky place in shallow seawater where oysters live.

- **SCHOOL:** A school of fish swims together. This helps fish to find mates and confuses enemies that can't decide which fish to eat!

- **SEA ANEMONE:** An anemone is a marine animal with no skeleton that looks like a colourful flower.

- **SEA COW (MANATEE or DUGONG):** This large, gentle sea creature is not a fish but a mammal, which comes to the surface for air. It lives in shallow waters and eats plants.

- **SEA HORSE:** The sea horse is among the tiniest fish in the coral reef. It can change colour to blend in with its surroundings. The males carry their babies in a pouch until the babies are big enough to care for themselves.

- **STARFISH:** Starfish live on the seabed and shore. They eat molluscs like mussels and clams, using the suction cups on their feet to pull the shells apart. Then they turn their stomachs inside out on top of their food to eat it.